# PILFERAGE
# OF THE CAVES

# PILFERAGE
# OF THE CAVES

Fiction

Based On

A Story Of Fractional Truths

By

Barbara Shaw Miller

# TABLE OF CONTENTS

# DEDICATION

This book would not have been written without the
inspiration, knowledge, and encouragement
given to me by the man I married and have
lived with for our 59 years together.

He has always been there when serious decisions
were needed to be made. He always encouraged
me to travel to different countries and to
learn from the experience.

These and many more recognitions
of his generous efforts to do the right thing is
Why I Dedicate
this book to the
LOVE OF MY LIFE :

CAPT. THOMAS J. MILLER USMC AVIATOR (Ret.)

# PREFACE

This story is set against the political and military realities of Central America amidst a not-too-distant backdrop of guerrilla warfare, intrigue, conspiracy, and murder.

It is a story of a young archeologist from Israel who along with a college friend from Guatemala became close friends sharing the joy of accomplishment whenever they became close to discoveries of unknown archeological artifacts located in the jungles of Central America.

Over the years they became more and more obsessed with a quest to discover one of the century's greatest archeological finds, ie., The Southern Classical Libraries of the Mayan culture and its civilization.

It was their passion to be able to be recognized as the "discoverers" of this valuable treasure and to be able to provide the world with a documentary of their discoveries.

This story evolved during the years of 1967 through 1980. History records during this time cycle that a civil war was carried on along the 200 kilometers of the common Guatemala and Honduras border with Nicaragua.

Over the years of their journey, they worked in cooperation with both Governments of Guatemala and Honduras. The Governments of Honduras and Guatemala agreed on many occasions that this major discovery would acknowledge that the archeologists involved were indeed the discoverers and they would have the authority to document and publicize this profound discovery.

The one caveat was that the discoveries needed to be confirmed and no one would be able to publicize the discovery of any Mayan treasure or announce to the world the identity of the valuable artifacts until the timing was appropriate.

At the time this made sense to the passionate archeologists since it was said that the Mayan caves were known to be well hidden and located in the hills of Honduras and Guatemala with most of the Mayan caves said to be in Honduras. As a result, this journey would be difficult and a lengthy one. They believed however with the governments support and their military assistance the doors to the jungles would be far easier to access.

Reportedly natives who traveled to the caves earlier described the artifacts in the caves within the Honduras centers to contain limestone carvings, jade sculptures, alabaster artifacts, and libraries. Many of the local natives, the Guerillas and most of the surrounding Tribes also told stories of their findings of the valuables.

The Governments of Guatemala and Honduras acted at that time to relocate the artifacts from their original location to hidden caves in either country's mountain areas.

This story was told to me by an elderly Spanish man, named Reyna Guzman who was hired by Mr. Charles Taylor (a Texas millionaire) said to have financed the Israeli's passion in Central America for decades.

He was hired by Mr. Taylor to verify that his story was as accurate as could be discovered. Reyna was hired because he had a favorable reputation as a Spaniard explorer expert in the history and culture of both countries that are so heavily involved with Mr. Taylor's story. As a longtime friend of Taylor's, Taylor respected Reyna's in-depth knowledge of the countries as well as the inner workings of their governments. More importantly he was a trustworthy long-time friend of Taylor.

I met Reyna in an established Mexican restaurant located south of Tucson Arizona, within the

Tucson airport vicinity. The restaurant just opened as I arrived. It was within a few minutes that I noticed a man whom I guessed was Reyna approaching. He was in his late 70s to possibly early 80s. He was a slim man, polite and seemingly shy. He was well dressed, clean white shirt, silver bolo tie, boots with silver tips and tan slacks. He spoke with a heavy Spanish accent which at times was difficult for me to understand.

After our introductions, I asked him who referred him to me? What did he expect to have me do for him? Where did he come from? Did he live in Arizona or was he from Mexico? He nervously answered my questions as he tightly held on to wrinkled papers that were obviously his notes, none of which were in English.

He said he was referred to me by an old-time mutual friend who lived in Tucson and died before we were able to meet. He apologized for not calling me sooner, but he was very concerned about telling this story to anyone. Whomever he met had to be trustworthy and willing to put this story in writing in English and hopefully publish it for all to see.

He contacted a lifetime friend in Tucson, AZ, named Julio Espinosa. Julio was the one person with whom Rayna would entrust his very life. Julio explained he had no way to publish this story, but he did remember someone whom he trusted and knew might have the right contacts to assist in getting this story told to the world.

Our mutual friend from Tucson was named Julio Espinosa. I remembered Julio but had not seen him for several years. Julio gave Reyna my phone number and suggested he contact me.

As time passed (even years) Reyna decided he needed to get this story told. He needed to meet with the best and safest person to discuss the information he collected as he said, "so justice could be served". This could possibly be his last visit to Mexico. He lived permanently in Guatemala and traveled from Guatemala through Mexico to Arizona.

He decided to make the call to me hoping my phone number would be correct. It was!!!! We spent an entire afternoon on the patio of this restaurant, being interrupted only by the occasional jet plane landing or taking off at the airport. At times a waiter would stop at the table and ask if we needed anything to drink or eat.

He went through his notes of what he discovered and encountered as he followed that path that was

originally taken by Mr. Taylor, including the results of his discoveries of Taylor's travels through Guatemala and Honduras. He also wanted Taylor's story told to the world not as told by Governments of Guatemala and Honduras, which in Reyna's opinion were not true.

Mr. Taylor wanted his story confirmed, and then released to the world for all to see. Taylor wanted the world to know and experience the pain and anguish his friends and himself suffered during the many trips made together over some 40 plus years. Mr. Taylor said it was Reyna's job to discover what was reality.

Were the many stories Taylor listened to during his exploring with the natives as well as the many stories told to him by the government officials in both Guatemala and Honduras told only to keep the truth of the Mayan artifacts from Taylor? Did Taylor and his Israeli friends lead the officials to the hidden caves whereupon they used this secret information for their own satisfaction?

Taylor often wondered where he went wrong, who took advantage of all his provisions, monetary and otherwise. He also wanted to know who, or which Government was in control of the discoveries in the long run. And finally, where did the artifacts disappear to? Where are they today? Countries? Museums? Private Investors? And/Or? Were they given as gifts or sold to anyone?

Mr. Taylor, a well-known lawyer from Texas, was a member of a prominent law firm family. Their law firm represented famous families and families of great wealth across the United States and around the world.

This story will describe the destruction of life, career, dignity, and ultimate progression of the Taylor family's inheritance. Charles Taylor financed this quest and ultimately his passion killed him. He died of an incurable disease, alone and in poverty. He cherished his dream but never experienced the joy of its reality.

Taylor spent 40 years in search for the origin of the Mayan archeological discoveries, the key which could unlock the mystery of one of the world's first great civilizations.

It was difficult at times to follow Reyna and clearly understand this Spanish man as he nervously and yet carefully wove his verbal and enigmatic mosaic of the special few who were obsessed with this discovery and as a result paid the ultimate price. He was hesitant at times to speak but he continually insisted that to follow in his path can be dangerous and so it is important to be careful and mindful of those who were and perhaps are involved with this part of the Mayan history and its historic discoveries.

Set forth is his story as best as I could understand and interpret. This Spanish gentleman insisted that his repeated investigations concluded and confirmed to be the truth as it was possible to be discovered.

Hours went by, and we suddenly realized it was dark and we both had to get on our way. Concluding, Reyna decided that all that needed to be known was told. There was no need to tell any more of this story.

We agreed all that was important had been said. He added, "please put this story in writing for Mr. Taylor's sake. He also reminded me once again that this could be a dangerous project.

We said our goodbyes and as we walked away from each other we both turned back to give one another a farewell glance. We shared a silent nod.

I never saw or heard from Reyna Guzman again.

# INTRODUCTION

During the time of this story happening a revolution in El Salvador and Nicaragua were deeply rooted. As a result, for years Guatemala and Honduras were in full defensive posture.

Since 1821, and their independence from Spain, these small nations endured wars, revolutions, coup-d'etat, earthquakes, volcanic eruptions, mysterious disappearances, political kidnappings, bombings, and assassinations in never ending cycles.

In 1965 the Honduras / El Salvador soccer war resulted in Guatemala siding (at least officially ) with El Salvador. This decision resulted in the two countries of Honduras and Guatemala at strong political odds with each other.

Throughout Central America civilian authority highly distrusted its military. The military totally distrusted all civilian authority. Add this to the above, the abject poverty, famine, oppression, over population, foreign intelligence interference, major government intimidation, and you have an overview of reality in Central America. It was total disaster.

Central America was an agrarian, a boiling caldron of armed guerilla factors. The military controlled the cities but not the countryside.

The campesianos (farmers) and Indian populations were caught in the crossfire. These natives were more fearful of the guerrillas in the countryside than the ruthless military which ventured there only on occasion.

Civilian atrocities are legend with each side overreacting with lethal force out of shear fear. Anyone who wasn't afraid was a fool, hopelessly naïve or both. Violence would erupt simultaneously in widely separated areas without respect for anything or anyone; all for which the machete was no match.

In 1561 A.D., Bishop Diego di Landa of the Spanish conquerors, burned 500 Mayan books and documents at Mani, Yucatan (Mexico).\, in a fit of Christian fervor. Many Mayans believed that he destroyed the entire Mayan culture's history.

Among the relics and artifacts of the Mayan civilization are tall, rectangular white stones known as stelae, engraved with highly stylized numbers.

It is believed that the Mayan people once stood in front of these artifacts and monuments chanting the names of their numbered gods, hoping to influence divine intervention in their lives. Each number was thought of as a god relating to particular characteristics and other aspects of human existence.

A thick lipped face, spotted with tattoos , is the god who depicted the number 2, symbolizing death and sacrifice. The wrinkled countenance of number 5 reminds us of the wisdom of age. In Mayan society these sacred numbers (rumored to be 150 in total) apparently made the passage of time possible for the number of gods are often depicted carrying the burden of the days, parceled out into units like hours and years, upon their backs.

Most famously are the Mayan Codices. These are screen fold books painted by Maya scribes before the Spanish conquest in the early 16th century pre-Columbian Mayan civilization. The Codices contain information about Mayan beliefs and rituals as well everyday activities all of which are found in the Astronomical and Calendrical content of the Maya civilization.

The Maya hieroglyphics were written by Maya scribes on Meso-American bark (inner bark) of certain trees.

Only three Mayan Codices, dated 1150 AD or later, are known to have survived. They are named after the cities in which they now repose: Paris, Madrid, and Dresden.

In 1970 however the Grolier was found. Reportedly, it is said to have been discovered in a cave in Honduras. Today it is in a museum in Mexico City. It is said its authenticity is still to be confirmed.

Mani is far from the ancient southern Mayan ceremonial centers, abandoned nine centuries earlier. It is unlikely Bishop Diego di Landa ever touched the southern classical libraries in which it is believed that the ancient Mayan, within a system of caves, periodically placed their most valuable artifacts to protect them and secure them from natural diseases, migrating from other conquering tribes as well as from the threat of communist control.

The native Indian tribes repeatedly told their stories that this location was one of the greatest closely guarded secrets for the past hundreds of years.

Honduras inadequately protected such a vast system of entrances to the caves along the border because of the demand on their military to protect their borders, fighting in the jungles against the guerillas and various tribes who were desperately protecting their villages against pilferaging, family killings, rape, and destruction of livelihood.

This was only in an effort to protect their borders. For centuries Honduras and Guatemala in particular have been very poor, and although they will do amazing things for their economy, they will not do so before they have control of their borders and eliminated the threat of communism from Cuba, Nicaragua, and El Salvador.

# CHAPTER I

# 1972

A rych Ben-Ami, an amateur archeologist and explorer, had visited Central America, especially Guatemala, many times over the past 15 years. He had explored, excavated, and searched the jungles, mountains, and savannas of the tropical Central American nations.

He believed he knew this part of the world as well as the natives. During this time, he became over-whelmed with a true passion to delve into the Mayan culture and more notably the caves which contained the hidden treasures of the Mayan civilization about which he had devoted years of studies.

Arych Ben-Ami's traveled several years throughout Central America, many of these sojourns throughout Central America were with his close friend of several years who retired in Guatemala Dr. David Epstein, also an educated archeologist, shared his passion for such discoveries.

Dr. Epstein phoned Arych one day and suggested that he board a plane and fly to Guatemala City. Dr. Epstein told him and described in detail several monoliths which Dr. Epstein had acquired. He then suggested that Arych drop everything and come to Guatemala City to examine several monoliths which Dr. David Epstein had collected.

He was certain that these monoliths depicted the Mayan dignitaries of the Classical era, he excitedly exclaimed to Arych, "This, of course, would be a very rare discovery in ancient American carvings."

In all there were three white limestone carved tablets averaging three feet in height, carved in low relief (bas relief) to be examined and investigated.

When asked where the monoliths were discovered, Dr. Epstein told Arych that he noticed a young Indian walking through the streets of Guatemala City one day with these monoliths on a wagon being pulled by a mule. He asked the Indian where did he get the carvings where-in he was told that they carved them at their workshop in the jungle. They would not explain further.

He was however willing to sell them to Dr. Epstein at a fair price. Of course, Dr. Epstein purchased the entire wagon load.

Arych said that he would catch a flight within the week and would plan to be in Guatemala as long as it takes to discover the origin of the monoliths purchased by Dr. Epstein.

# CHAPTER II

# DR. EPSTEIN

Dr. Epstein watched as the TWA plane from Tel-Aviv, Israel circled the airport. It arrived as scheduled. Finally, the plane approached the runway and landed at The international airport in Guatemala City.

He was thrilled to see his friend step off the plane and walk toward the terminal. He watched as Arych walked toward him. He had forgotten how tall and good looking Arych was. He thought for a second, "he could be a male model."

They greeted each other with broad smiles, hugs, and lots of laughter. They joked about their matching white shirts implying they were attempting to look like a native and not a tourist. It was interesting to see the two walking together. Arych at 5'11" and David at approximately 5'9" in heights.

They exited the airport after recovering Arych luggage from the baggage claim area. As they walked to the parking lot in front of the main entrance to the airport, they chatted about the beautiful weather, just as Arych remembered. Dr. Epstein suggested that this weather was for his arrival. He also pointed to the palm trees which were swaying to a chorus put on to welcome Arych.

As they stood in amazement that they were actually together neither one sensed the sinister, violent nature of the political reality of this coffee/banana republic.

They went directly to Dr. Epstein's apartment where he was keeping the monoliths under lock and key allowing no one to know of their existence. They were both eager to begin their evaluations of these monoliths. Interestingly, Dr. Epstein doubted their authenticity. But as they continued to study every inch of the monoliths Arych felt there was something significant in the tablets specifically in their preservation. For one he believed the tablets lacked the normal weathering and patina.

In depth discussions then began between the two as they pondered their findings. Two questions came to mind: (1) were they the product of modern manufacturing or (2) indeed were they sheltered artifacts?

It was decided that the only remaining solution was to remove the artifacts from the country to have them evaluated by an expert in the archeological field either in the USA or in a European country like Paris or Germany.

In order to do this however it required the approval of the Director of Archeology at The Department of Archeology of Guatemala. The Director was a prominent archeologist named Dr. Pedro Artemio. Their appointment was made, and they were scheduled for that very afternoon.

Upon meeting Dr. Artemio they went into detail on their reasoning these tablets were being altered. Arych described the testing that he and Dr. Epstein put the pieces through to authenticate. Their studies also concluded that these types of pieces were unknown in Guatemala. They also then noticed that there were metal tool marks on the surface and along the edges. The markings varied from piece to piece.

It was known that the Mayans did not have nor were known to have metal tools and that these tablets were also whitewashed in appearance which removed any patina or staining resulting in age.

They therefore determined these discoveries were and had to be copies. Dr. Artemio was quite silent during this meeting. His questions were simple and appeared to have no thought behind them.

Arych was puzzled by Dr. Artemio's reaction. Arych mind traveled to one question which he silently asked himself a question, "How did anyone reproduce an unpublished artifact?"

Finally, Dr. Artemio granted them permission to export them out of the country to an archeologist for study. They were to be identified as copies being exported for detailed studies. They were completely approved for shipment without further question or investigation by the airport authorities.

# CHAPTER III

# THE MONOLITHS

Arych thought of an old friend who lived in Dallas, Texas, a well-known archeologist whom he believed could be trusted to conduct the appropriate tests on the monoliths.

During most of the meeting with the Director, Arych watched his expression closely. Director Artemio did not comment during this meeting. He did not appear to be surprised just cautiously intent as they continued to discuss the monoliths and look them over closely.

It was then Arych began to notice that the monoliths were constructed by a limestone that he believed could be ancient. Arych held his breath, as he secretly began to realize and to believe that the basic limestone from which the tablets (monoliths) were fashioned to be millions of years old.

As Arych and Dr. Epstein left Dr. Artemio's office, Arych began to share his secret beliefs with Dr. Epstein. He told him how he believed that the basic limestone from which the tablets were fashioned to be millions of years old. He said that during their meeting Arych began to realize that these monoliths actually showed affirmatively that they were sculptured by hand using with stone tools. Indeed, he was now certain that the metal markings and whitewash was added much later after the original carving.

At this time there were no available laboratory tests to determine age of the stone carvings except for hydration testing of Obsidian Sculptures and thermoluminescence testing of certain fired clay pieces. Any sculpture at this time on animal or plant matter, such as carving on bone or wood lintels, would be considered carbon -14 dated. Carbon-14 is a convincing way to determine age of archeological artifacts. Whereas stone is in a gray stage.

Arych was fully aware that it actually frightens archeologists to be asked to render a date for a stone sculpture because they can easily be discredited professionally. In their minds it is safer to deny authenticity for all stone sculptures than to have a verifiable unquestioned history. The more he thought, the more he decided to immediately call his friend, who was also the curator at the museum in Dallas, Texas.

Arych explained that he thought further about the monoliths and decided before exporting them to Dallas he personally wanted to do more in depth investigation before he sent the sculptures to his attention.

Arych was an Israeli citizen, but he also had become a citizen of the United States. He decided not to return to either country at this time but to remain in Guatemala City in order to continue to trace the monoliths origins.

He and Dr. Epstein placed the monoliths in safe storage while they continued to ascertain if the monoliths held historical significance and were indeed unpublished artifacts. He decided that he and he alone would undertake searching for their origin.

He discussed this with Dr. Epstein and they both agreed that the doctor would remain in Guatemala City retaining an apartment and a room for Arych to live during his time in Guatemala City and it would be available to him as long as he was In Guatemala.

Dr. Epstein would also keep an alert eye on the monoliths and be aware of any additional monoliths appearing on the streets of Guatemala City.

Arych needed to discover who was placing them on the market and who was altering them with modern tools and whitewash.

# CHAPTER IV

# RUMORS

Over the next two years Arych followed many rumors from the streets of Guatemala City as to who was selling monoliths and/or other artifacts that could be associated with the Mayan culture.

He made several trips in the remote areas of Guatemala. Using guides to show him the way. He traveled through many remote areas of the country. He macheted his way through sections of tropical rain forests even crossing the border of Honduras entering into the dense woods and difficult mountainous northwestern areas.

Along the way many of the guides refused to continue on their way especially as they approached the border of Honduras. Arych questioned "why"? It seems rumor that all who entered this region did not return alive – did not return at all.

He followed rumor after rumor, one lead after another. He searched cave after cave being tossed around on the narrow dirt paths which the guides called roads. They were extremely narrow, and snake like in design as they hugged the edge of the mountain. One slip and Arych thought he was done for. Arych pushed the guides to go deeper and deeper into the jungle.

They continually explained to go further would mean having to fight the Gorillas or the various Indian tribes who were ruthlessly protective of their territory.

The Indian guides did not hesitate to take his money, but it was surely feeling like he was on a merry-go-round. He was beginning to realize that these guides were enjoying the ride and taking him to the cleaners.

His life was at risk every second. The Indians and Latinos led him into areas they claimed had not been seen by a human being before. He watched the primitive way these tribes lived as naked breast women bare footed, carrying their water pots on their heads while carrying their babies on their backs. He saw corpse after corpse as they walked along muddy paths. The Indians it seemed had no respect for the dead let along for the living.

Latinos led him into hostile areas with no means of defense. Frequently they did not supply water or even sufficient food for Arych or any of his trusted guides. Arych suddenly realized that their medicine and drugs were being tampered. He asked about it and they did nothing but laugh at him.

Arych always planned to return to Guatemala City at least every so many weeks or he would send a guide back to return with clean clothing, food, medicine, etc. But on the whole, they continued their trek throughout the lush rain forests throughout the mountains of Guatemala and Honduras.

Arych decided it was time to take a break and return to Guatemala City to catch up on the news with Dr. Epstein as well as to get some needed rest. He would venture forth once again in a month or two.

During this visit with Dr. Epstein, they heard of a group of adventurers who described their visit to a village close to the Guatemala and Honduras border where they found pieces of limestone and other materials that could be described as coming from one of the caves. True or not Arych immediately prepared to venture forth into their path.

Arych began to prepare for his next trip. He hired his trustworthy guides and since he was told that he would have to cross white water to reach one of the villages as described by the natives he purchased a canoe. The canoe was made of heavy weather and water resistance wood, deep enough to hold many days of supplies as well as Arych and three of his guides. The canoe trip was necessary in order to reach one of the villages described by the guides as a village at the bottom of a high mountain with several waterfalls flowing out of the mountain.

They convinced Arych that this location was where the carvings were coming from. The adventurers told Arych they estimated it would take 3 weeks to get to any one of the villages. As they pushed along the trail, Arych became ill. He became feverish and was unable to keep anything in his stomach and he felt he was on the verge of hypothermia. He was close to death.

Along the river they came across a small village of Indians who were trying to make a living and stay alive while evading the guerrillas as well as the angry farmers. The villagers greeted the canoe and without hesitancy took Arych into one of their small huts and built a fire to warm him.

Their "medicine" man began to treat him with certain oils and other methods of healing. Arych was in bad shape and all around him suspected that he would not make it out alive and it would not be long before he died. The guides thought that the only reason he was still alive was his determination to discover the Mayan artifacts that he vowed he would not die before he was successful in becoming the discover of the history of the lost Mayan.

One evening as the fever began to pass, Arych opened his eyes. He looked around the hut and then stared at the fire burning in the center. Suddenly through the flames he saw a beautiful lady walking toward him.

She had long black hair; eyes of deep dark pools of blue. He was able to see her quite clearly though the light of the fire. She was young maybe in her late teens or early twenties. At first, he thought he died and went to heaven, and she was an angel sent by God to escort him home. She moved toward him. She had a small bowl in her hands. As she got next to him, she knelt beside him, and he realized she was about to feed him.

After she slowly fed him, she began to wipe his brow and carefully began to massage his arms and shoulders. She smiled at him and seemed so happy that he was awake. She spoke little English, and he did not recognize the language she spoke. Together however they seem to manage to make conversation using their eyes and hands. They began to laugh and giggle at literally nothing. They did manage to exchange names; he was to call her Eylea.

Arych looked forward to each day and to Eylea's visits. More and more he studied her beauty. Her breasts were always uncovered and Arych could not help but become excited over their youthful shape.

He began to wonder what she looked like completely naked. Bad boy, he thought to himself. Surely his emotions were obvious. They both realized this desire to become one was not only mutual but so strong it would not be long before they were one. No doubt all this signaled his health problems would soon be over and he could be on his way.

She visited frequently. With each visit they became closer and closer. One day Arych sat up and pulled her to him. He smiled as if to ask permission to move forward. She smiled back as if to say "yes". This act of love was sincere, and each had so much enjoyment. It went on all evening.

For days ahead they continued their tryst and Arych was at a point where he might not even to go forward. But love does not conquer all. This went on for three weeks. Finally, it was time to make the inevitable decision. The Natives were anxious to move forward and continue this journey. They healed him back to health and he was appreciative. They lost considerable time. They were given food and some water from the river to help them on their way. Eylea tearfully hugged and kissed Arych. He too felt as if he was about to lose his most precious possession. He explained to Eylea that this journey was far too dangerous for her to travel with him. He also promised that on the trip returning to Guatemala City he would be certain to stop and get her and take her back to

Guatemala City with him. He asked her to wait and without hesitation she told him she would.

One day of their journey as they trekked through the thick brush and hacked their way to an open area in a remote location near the frontier of the Guatemala and Honduras border Arych came across limestone tracks and as such determined that this location has to be where the monoliths originated.

His group and their mules hiked along dangerous dirt roads along the ridges of high mountains (he wished he were a mule). Their path took them across deep mud flows. Mountains so densely treed that one could only make out a path by looking up and following the tall trees that appeared to be a path. When it was impossible to continue, they pulled out their machetes and chopped trees and brush down sized enough for them to pass.

From afar they could hear Indians and farmers checking them out following as it were as they trudged along. At one point they were approached by guerrilla warriors who demanded their food and wanted their weapons. They fought with them and lost giving up most of their food and several of their machetes. Arych had hidden well his machete and his small pocket gun which he always carried but kept hidden from everyone. They continued on their journey to locate this particular village as told often in Guatemala City as the one village that produced the carved Monoliths. Arych was determined more than ever that they push forward.

Now they were hungry and exhausted, but this was not going to stop them since they sensed they were getting closer to their objective. A few days passed. They eluded several warriors by being alert to the fact that they existed and were well camped in this territory. When the sun appeared, they could see it reflecting off the machete blade of the warriors which warned them of the enemy persistently following and surrounding them as they pushed forward. However, as they pushed forward those following them became nervous that they were walking directly into the villages that most feared.

So, they retreated.

# CHAPTER V

# POCO SANCHEZ

They finally arrived at the top of a mountain where several mountain streams flowed with crystal clear water. From this location they were able to see a good distance all around. Most importantly they saw below at the foot of this mountain the thatched roof huts of a small village. It appeared to be inhabited with a tribe consisting of a few families.

The huts were built in a circle around a cleared center which he surmised was used for activities such as meetings, eating, and entertainment. People were going in different directions. From the distance, they were not certain if this would be a hostile village but they had no choice except to approach it and meet the people.

Arych's guides identified them as that of the Mestiso Indians. They did not openly welcome Arych and his guides but remained silent and hidden until their

Chief announced it would be safe to show themselves to these strangers. Thus, it was now thought that this village would be friendly and not ready to take Arych and his team to task. The village was utter poverty; poorly developed in fact not developed at all. As he witnessed on other treks over the past year the women carried water from the foot of the mountain into the village in hand made vessels on their heads; children were dirty but playing in the area, laughing since it was obvious, they knew no better. Old and young alike sat in the grass or on the dirt. They sat with their knees bent in a crouched position so that the only part of their body that touched the ground were their feet. Old men and women were smoking but what it was Arych could not determine.

Many were tattooed with different designs. Arych wondered what these signs meant. He did not recognize them as Mayan tattoos, but he just wasn't sure.

A young Indian who came forth to meet them and ask what it was they wanted. He told them their village was called "Jocotan." Arych proceeded to described the monoliths and asked if the Indian was aware of such artifacts. The young man then claimed to be the creator of the tablets, in fact, admitted that once he carved them, he would take them to Guatemala City and sell them to tourist and on occasion to art dealers seeking ancient artifacts. Arych was elated for he now knew he found the Indian who sold the mono-liths to Dr. Epstein.

This was the same man.

This man was called Poco Sanchez. After the intro-ductions Poco announced to the Indian Tribe to pre-pare a feast in the village for the men who arrived. They would sit in the evening and smoke together as well as enjoy their food and entertainment. They were given a hut for the men to sleep, and they slept well on palm fronds.

In the morning the men awoke and were met with a buffet of breakfast foods. After that, Poco invited Arych to his hut where he said they could talk about the monoliths. They moved into Poco's hut and sat in a poorly lit room surrounded by men heavily tat-tooed but who appeared to be totally bewildered. The two men talked for hours with Arych asking many questions while Poco hemmed and hawed avoiding answers.

Poco declared that his home was his workshop. However, Arych saw no evidence of equipment, art-work, or any other evidence that this was a workshop to create such monoliths. He did however come upon two small carved tablets just outside leaning against the hut. Arych examined the two tablets carefully and he noted that these stones had patina but no sign of weathering. Poco was a poor liar and apparently a successful entrepreneur but not the artist he professed to be.

Poco admitted to having no training in art. He claimed he created the tablets from his imagination. He claimed that he never visited a Mayan Museum, nor did he ever see or read a book on ancient Maya. Arych asked if he could watch Poco create and process his creations. Poco was quick to say "NO". Poco said the method was a secret process.

Once again Arych took a good look around his home, his workshop. No pictures, books, drawings, sculpting or quarry tools, forklift, hoist, truck were anywhere in the vicinity of this workshop.

There was no evidence of work in progress and no evidence of an ability to create such a process. Arych played along with Poco and since Arych had no choice in the matter under these conditions, he played Poco's game, and he heeded Poco's rules.

Arych and Poco spent several days negotiating a contract to have Poco create similar pieces from his imagination for Arych. The first shipment would be 50 pieces and would be ready in approximately five weeks. Arych promised a bonus if Poco could deliver this order within three weeks. Poco quickly replied this would be impossible, but he would do his best to honor their agreement.

# CHAPTER VI

# THE INTERVIEWS

A rych packed up, gathered his guides, and hired a few members of the tribe to escort his return to Guatemala City. Poco told him that the way they came across the mountain was a very long way and that there was an easier way to travel as Poco and his villagers did. Poco was correct, the return route was faster than the route taken to get to the village as guided by the team of men who apparently knew better.

Arych's disappointment was that he would not be able to get to Eylea's village and bring her back to Guatemala City with him as promised. He vowed to himself that he would return to her as soon as he was able to get this sale process with Poco started.

Upon his return to Guatemala City, he and Dr. Epstein began to interview private detectives. Arych did not believe Poco and knew that he had a scheme to secure the artifacts, whitewash them and alter their outward appearance so they looked like replicas.

Poco is clever and he needs watching. He needed someone to figure Poco's process out. He wanted someone with a background of operations in Central America, someone who understood tribal cultures, and someone who knew how to play the political game in Central America.

Most applicants did not satisfy either Arych or David. Owen, a former personal bodyguard to the President appeared one day to be interviewed. He had a permit to carry a .45 military pistol in his belt. He was a tall, intimidating man, who was in his mid-thirties. He was immediately hired, and his name was Eli Manual. He was given a two-week assignment to travel to Jocotan to see how he conducted himself on such a journey and to see what he could discover.

During his time near the village Eli watched village youths hiking into the mountains, entering caves only at night and returning immediately to the rear entrance of Poco's hut, dropping off monoliths as Poco paid them for each piece. Eli was from this region and had a large family in this part of the Country.

Over time, he witnessed murder and violence and knew as rumors spread of the money being paid for the monoliths that it would not be long before jealously, greed, violence and murder would soon become more commonplace in and around the village of Jocotan.

The young people were becoming more and more aware of the money Poco was earning and they were beginning to want a bigger share. They began killing each other for larger shares and a favorable place in line to be assigned to enter the caves to secure the monoliths and then to get paid. The result was more murder and violence among the families who would not cooperate to assist them to earn their share of Poco's secret.

Having family and relatives so close to this brought fear to Eli for his family and himself. He decided to return to Guatemala City and immediately went to visit Arych whereupon he explained in detail what was occurring in Jocotan and the surrounding villages. He went into detail of his fear for his family and unsafe he believed for him as well to continue to spy on Jocotan. He resigned from his assignment with Arych. His intent was to return to his village and quickly move his family away from the dangers they faced and how he saw what that danger was.

At this final meeting with Arych and Dr. Epstein, Eli showed him daily newspaper articles reporting about the number of bodies found in the rural farm communities, all to the southwest of the village of Jocotan. This more than supported Eli's reason for resigning from his assignment with Arych. As Eli told of these stories, Arych was witnessing all this fear in his eyes. This clearly brought home to him the reality of this early discovery of the unpublished subterranean sanctuary caused the caves to be robbed and looted of its ancient artifacts.

It was after this meeting with Eli that Dr. Epstein told Arych that he would need care since he was diagnosed with cancer and was given a limited time to live. Needless to say, this upset Arych very much. He told Dr. Epstein that he would do whatever he could to get this journey successfully done so that Dr. Epstein would live to see their accomplishments.

They quietly continued their visit discussing further that as time and gossip spread the rumors told of entire ancient libraries having been discovered in the caves originally of subterranean Mayan centers. Of course, they each decided that this now explains the condition of the tablets. They were not weathered or eroded by the elements as were most stelae carvings which have withstood the elements over centuries in the jungle and mountains.

# CHAPTER VII

# 50 PIECES

Poco Sanchez had access to a telegraph used by the warriors, and he occasionally communicated with Guatemala City this way. Arych received a telegram wire three weeks to the day from Poco that the shipment was ready. The thought did occur to Arych that it was interesting to hear that Poco had access to a telegraph and with the guerrilla warriors yet!

The very next morning Arych rented a 4-wheel drive, a truck. and drove with two trustworthy natives to Jocotan. Nonstop it would take him at least 3 days.

He could hardly speak when he saw the carvings. All 50 pieces were exquisite. All 50 pieces were spread out on the ground surrounding Poco's workshop.

Arych paid Poco their agreed price and a bonus for the early delivery. It was now up to Arych to get the monoliths in authentic condition to Guatemala

City. Unfortunately, the bad news now, is that the money Arych paid to Poco was just about all he had left at this time.

The good news is that Arych is now convinced that Poco was not the creator of the tables. Arych had now solved one of the mysteries of the monoliths.

Arych was so excited that he was finally on the path of accomplishment. Unfortunately, Dr. Epstein was not here at this side to relish the good news.

# CHAPTER VIII

# LATE 1974 ~ 1975

With Dr. Epstein's passing and his need to earn money, Arych gathered the monoliths and placed them in storage for safety. He had no choice since he needed money to cover all expenses to ship the monoliths out of the country. He spent a good portion of the first part of the year working at odd jobs and repaying the amounts of money he was borrowing i.e., borrowing from Peter to pay Paul.

Finally in November of year 1974 he located one of the street people living just outside the City who were described by Eli as a knowledgeable guide. In particular one known as Angus was particularly aware of the ancient subterranean caves and whom he and Eli before him had been searching for months. Angus and Eli spoke of the looting and murders in the village of Jocotan.

His story goes back a good seven years earlier. It tells of the tribes killing to capture the artifacts from those removing them from the caves. They were then delivering them to Poco. In return he would pay them a wage.

This rumor had now become Arych's main thrust to many frustrating expeditions. The street people named the looting and killings as The Dr. Julio Lopez Story.

As the story goes, they cited that in 1967 three men: a retired American doctor, an Indian hunting guide and a German National, had tricked a Mayan descendent into leading them to an obscure entrance of a highly secret and sacred ancestral site in a remote area along the Guatemala Honduran border.

These were huge razorback mountains with the ruins of an observatory on one's peak, huge carved stelae on its slopes and a white limestone quarry at its base from which flowed 5 small mountain streams. The entrance was obscured by the dense forest in the quebrada (ravine) which is two-thirds of the way to the summit.

The men hired a pilot to fly and land a helicopter on the mountain and stayed on the mountain for a period of two months making one and sometimes two flights a day with artifacts aboard. The men paid a tribal Indian from a nearby Spanish farm, (known as a finca) to bring them food and water each evening.

One day and the tribal Indian went to the mountain top to bring them the daily food and water, he was quite taken back for, as he reported to the tribe, the men and the helicopter had suddenly left the mountain. He also noted that the German National's body was lying on the ground dead, he was beheaded, allegedly by the rotary blades of the helicopter, he thought. However, others in the tribe said the wounds appeared similar to those of a machete.

Arych having heard this story hurried to meet with Dr. Lopez, the retired American doctor in Guatemala City where the doctor had lived for several years. They spent well over several hours with Arych listening attentively to the Doctor's story which included a detailed description of the site and its contents. Dr. Lopez included descriptions of codices (Mayan Manuscripts). All this time going into detail about the cave and the discoveries, he never disclosed the general location of the site he so proudly discussed.

Arych was now convinced that Poco was merely fronting for the theft of these treasures which came from the mountain sanctuary looted by Dr. Lopez and his Guatemalan Indian partner, Grade. This quest for Arych had taken on the magnitude of discovering the equivalent of the Dead Sea Scrolls. He was now certain he would find the source of the Mayan treasures. However, by now Arych was indeed out of money. He silently continued to collect clues and preserve them for his eventual publication as well as for a documentary on the subject. His primary interest was to be known as the man who discovered the untold mystery.

# CHAPTER IX

# CHARLES TAYLOR

A rych's burning need to continue was hampered by the fact that he was out of money. He decided it was time to bring in an investment partner and so he contacted an old friend in Texas.

Charles Taylor was a wealthy attorney and a prominent art collector living in Dallas. He told Charles of this quest and his belief that he would indeed find the missing libraries of the ancient Mayan civilization. He explained that this discovery could revolutionize and possibly rewrite the pre-history of the Americas, perhaps even trace one or more of the lost tribes of Israel.

He continued to entice Taylor's attention with the various possibilities such as pharmaceutical achievements of the ancients which are contained in their writings. This could conceivably cure diseases effecting society. The libraries might contain facts relative to the origins of the earliest people to inhabit the Americas, their integrations, migrations, and demise.

Charles Taylor was a member of a prominent family whose law firm was legendary in the state of Texas. He inherited his father's law practice, wealth, network of astute businessmen, art dealers, and collectors in the International marketplace. Charles offered to schedule a meeting for Arych with Antiquities dealers in Texas to see if he could bring investment dollars to Arych's research. His travel arrangements were made to visit Dallas where all of the important and wealthy contacts could come together to listen to Arych's story and of his quest.

The meetings were very successful. Heavy monetary investments were made to Arych based upon Arych's belief that the true source would be publicly acclaimed shortly. The investors would each be honored for their participation in this journey.

Over the next 18 months Arych and his newly found partner Charles Taylor began to travel in pursuit of clues. They traveled to Guatemala City together and Arych arranged for them both to meet with Dr. Lopez and Grade, Dr. Lopez' Indian guide. Dr. Lopez suggested that if they paid all expenses including the helicopter, he would escort them to the site.

Meanwhile, Arych and Poco continued to play their game. Arych and Taylor changed their buying habits ordering specific pieces to be delivered to them in Guatemala City. Poco was not able to deliver the larger tablets. His biggest fear was that he would not be able to secure the permit for them to get the tablets out of the country. He asked that Arych go to the Director of Archeology to get permission to remove the larger tablets from the country. If Arych could get approval and the permit, then Poco would deliver the larger tablets.

Once again Arych visited with Dr. Artemio, Director of the Department of Archeology in Guatemala City. And once again he repeated to Dr. Munoz that these tablets were coming from the mountain caves near Jocotan, and he did not believe the stories as told by Poco. With this repeated explanation Dr. Artemio had a good laugh as Arych continued his belief of the tablets origin. Dr. Artemio issued the required permits which listed the tablets and other artifacts as copies.

The tablets now could be listed for exportation. Dr. Artemio however never mentioned that he and his government were watching Arych and his operation closely and perhaps for devious reasons.

Poco continued his deliveries, six large tablets in one shipment and 8 large tablets in another to a facility in Guatemala City. From April through December of 1975, Arych continued to trace the carvings back to Jocotan.

They varied in sizes from 60 pounds upwards to one ton. These shipments contained ball court markers, giant hieroglyphic texts, calendars of the 260-day religious and the 365-day solar, sculptures of astronomers, religious figures, historical personages and stone heads.

All the carvings were inspected and released for shipment as copies. All were similar. Arych and Taylor cooperated with the Guatemalan authorities with every shipment. They cooperated with the authorities although at times they did not understand why the authorities needed certain information for which they asked. They continued to maintain that the pieces were altered artifacts.

# ELI MANUAL

In November 1975, Arych and Charles met with Eli Manual and asked him to revisit the area where he observed the stones were being looted by the youths of the village.

He refused. After further discussion and with the bounty increase to a point where Eli could not refuse, he said yes that he would go to Jocotan. He did remind Arych that the tablets were not being made in Jocotan but were coming from the mountain caves which is now surrounded by terrorists and guerrillas fighting to the death over the artifacts in the Caves.

Before the week ended Arych received word that Eli's body was discovered on a coffee plantation located near the mountain just south of the frontier village of Jocotan.

Poco delivered 240 carvings weighing thousands of pounds. With such frequency that Arych and Charles became nervous that others might discover that Poco was not the artist, and that any investigation would have to end at Jocotan. It was then that they decided to make Poco a partner and to form a company in Guatemala City.

# CHAPTER XI

# 1976

They proceeded to sign agreements and then to file all the necessary papers with the government. They then ordered stationery and business cards as well as to lease a workshop. By the end of January 1976 Poco was officially set up to do carving business in his factory in Jocotan acting as partners to Dr. Epstein and Arych Ben-Ami.

This plot, devised by Arych was to demonstrate to Poco how to powder the limestone and fill the carvings until the surface was smooth. At this point Poco was to then carry the carvings through the village for all to see, supposedly bringing this material to his shop for him to do the carving.

Once he got every item in his shop, he would brush off the loose material and then deliver the tablets to Arych and Taylor.

During the years of research and living in Guatemala City, Arych made many friends including a Colonel with the Guatemalan Air Force, Colonel Richard Symth. They frequently met for lunch or dinner and drank together on many occasions. They enjoyed many stories of the events that happened to Guatemala, Guatemala City, and the surrounding countries over the past decades. They spoke often about Arych's tablets and Arych's observation of the tablets authenticity. Arych also discussed that he felt the site where the tablets were coming from was part of an undiscovered ancient complex. He made his judgment based upon the variety and various styles of the artifacts.

In early February of 1976 Guatemala was struck with an earthquake that ripped apart major roadways, bridges, and dams. Colonel Symth was sent into the area to use their newest form of high-level aerial infra-red cameras in order for the government of Guatemala to estimate the extent of the damage.

Upon his return to Guatemala City, Colonel Symth immediately called Arych. "You were right," he exclaimed. Our surveillance flights revealed an unusually large lineal intrusion just east of Jocotan. This ran near the Montagua Valley in Guatemala, between the Ulua Valley in Honduras and Quirigua, Guatemala, near the El Salvador frontier. Changes in colors in the photos indicated that there is multiple series of caves and underground spaces.

Colonel Symth felt it was imperative that they meet with Colonel Alberto Lemos who is head of Internal Security and is in the President's Cabinet. Colonel Symth then went on to report to Arych that he had a preliminary discussion with Colonel Lemos about this discovery. He was most anxious to visit with Arych and to learn all about his findings in these mountains.

Arych was pleased to hear this. He believed that with the government behind his discovery he could go public officially within days, weeks, certainly within a few months. It is to be the largest archeological discovery in the history of the Americas.

Oh, he was so wrong. The two Colonels met with Arych and with Dr. Artemio. The discussion was about the differences of opinion of Arych's who believed the tablets were authentic and Dr. Artemio who believed Arych was crazy. How could anyone be sane and believe these tablets came from an ancient subterranean sanctuary. They would have to travel to the caves to prove who is sane and who is not.

Colonel Lemos feared any travel into the Jocotan area. He especially would be a prime victim for the guerrillas and bandidos. At this time violence, intrigue, murder, death squads, communist insurgents, kidnappings fire fights, ambushes, and conspiracies were growing rapidly more so each week.

However, Lemos decided in reality he could help Arych to get to the truth by interrogating Poco and then possibly Poco would lead them to the entrances to the caves and show them the depth of the tunnels.

Colonel Lemos then suggested that he would provide a special military unit to escort Arych when he visits Poco in Jocotan. If Poco is carving stones, they would need to know where the quarry was located.

Arych then immediately jumped on the idea since with such support Arych could discover the location where Poco got his sources of Stones he said to be carving.

# CHAPTER XII

# JOCOTAN QUARRY

Arych traveled to Jocotan with a military escort. He explained what he wanted to Poco. Poco took the group, and they climbed the mountains. On one particular mountain he showed Arych several holes. Naturally this was quite a disappointment since there should be hundreds of holes and a quarry.

Conclusion: There was no Jocotan quarry.

After a few days Colonel Symth decided to contact Poco directly and invite him to visit Guatemala City and to bring along two of his aides so that they could carve a stone in their presence. We want to witness you at work on your carvings, he said. Poco agreed and soon arrived to meet Colonel Symth. Poco arrived with an uncarved stone, and they proceeded to work with great effort to carve – with their results so primitive there was no way their work could be identified with the tablets Poco sold to Arych.

Colonel Symth was now totally convinced that Arych was correct. He suggested that they take a military helicopter and fly around the mountains. They could concentrate on the particular area cited by the surveillance cameras. Arych, Charles Taylor, and the Colonel spent the day flying over Jocotan searching for cave openings. Eventually they spotted a large opening and they circled it several times seeking a proper location to land the helicopter safely.

As they began to approach their designated landing site, Arych suddenly saw someone moving in the cave opening. He sensed danger for the helicopter and its passengers. He immediately shouted, "take off, "don't land, get us out of here!"

The pilot of this helicopter immediately turned the craft around and flew it to Zacapa, a military base, where they could refuel for the return trip to Guatemala City. The very next day while another helicopter from Zacapa was on military patrol, it was reported that dozens of armed guerrillas were seen leaving this exact cave and they reported they were moving their base of operation since they believed they had been discovered.

Colonel Lemos sent a unit of Guatemala commandos into this area where the commandos found themselves battling with hundreds of communist guerrillas. This battle went on for several weeks. The

Guatemalan army would not give up and pursued the guerrillas right through the maze of caves which ultimately revealed that the caves were inter-connected directly into the territory of Honduras.

During this fighting, Colonel Symth was hospitalized in the military hospital in Guatemala City with a relapse of malaria. As it is told, the same pilot who flew Arych, Charles and the Colonel also flew several wounded military soldiers from this battlefield to the same military hospital. The pilot met with Colonel Symth and hurried to tell him the stories of the vast treasures the soldiers had seen in the subterranean complex.

During this same time Poco was being interrogated by the Guatemala police for fraud. Poco Sanchez would not tell them anything. The fear for his life went far beyond the threats made by the police.

Upon his recovery Colonel Symth immediately contacted Arych and told him of the discovery during all of the military battles at the location of the caves. He said that Colonel Lemos wanted both of them to attend a meeting with him the very next day.

Once again Arych rejoiced thinking this discovery would be over and he could return to Israel. Arych was not interested in the artifacts for sale, he only wanted recognition for discovering the cave and the treasures. It had been some time since he saw his elderly parents. He strongly believed that he was nearing the end of this journey, he believed he was at the end of this intense, dangerous search.

Once again, he was wrong.

# CHAPTER XIII

# COLONEL LEMOS

During the weeks that Colonel Symth was in the hospital and the troops were invading the area, many were killed and kidnapped in Jocotan. The Guatemala government started its collection of suspected looters. The government also arrested anyone considered to be an antiquities dealer. Many innocent suspects or not went to prison to protect Colonel Lemos.

Colonel Lemos asked Colonel Symth and Arych to treat this meeting with the upmost of secrecy. A stern-faced Colonel Lemos began to tell the related events of the battle, how the prisoners in the caves were tortured. He told of their wonderment when the helicopter suddenly turned around and flew away, that it was the precise time the guerrillas were set to fire upon the helicopter destroying it and all on board.

Colonel Lemos related how the military troops pursued the guerrillas through the mountains and through the vast unending cave system which went to ten kilometers into the sovereign territory of Honduras. He told of how the countries were not on speaking terms, but that Honduran military were working closely with the Guatemalan troops to clear up the area. He confirmed being told that there were 16 subterranean centers filled with art treasures of the ancient temples of unbelievable size and the carvings were beyond description. There were libraries of considerable size in each cave. Two of the caves were looted but the total ancient ceremonial centers counted were eighteen. Arych sat in awe and in disbelief. He remembered the ridicule he underwent by the archeologists and of course the Guatemalan Department of Archeology.

Colonel Lemos stressed the fact that this was now a military matter, and they were not to reveal any of this information to anyone until permission could be given by the military. This was a matter for internal security, and it was especially not to be told to anyone in the Department of Archeology.

Now what was Arych to do? These orders were coming from those who run the country. These are the people who grant or deny entry, permits and/or worse.

Colonel Lemos told Arych that only a few of the cave centers are within the territory of Guatemala, most of the centers are within Honduras. However, the military had signed a pact with Honduras to not publicize this discovery until all was ready. With the war in existence among Nicaragua and Guatemala and with a communist threat in El Salvador, there was no choice but to wait. Colonel Lemos suggested that Arych could begin all over once again by meeting with the authorities in Honduras. He told Arych that the site he needed to enter was Cerro El Bonete, eleven kilometers south of the ruins of Copan.

Colonel Lemos reviewed with Arych the years of 1967 and 1968 when the carvings were removed from the cave to avoid looting and re-hidden to preserve them from natural disasters. Colonel Lemos said goodbye to Arych giving him the coordinates for the proper contact in the government of Honduras.

Colonel Lemos put his arm around Arych's shoulder and walked out of the offices of Internal Security. Arych quickly noted that Colonel Lemos' office is located directly next to the President's office. They had coffee and continued their discussion for another hour. By the time Arych returned to his apartment, his head was spinning. He could not have dinner; he was not hungry. He was so excited, he immediately called Charles Taylor. He told Taylor to immediately fly down to Guatemala City to visit.

Arych said, "It won't be long now. I have now iden-tified the site, but I cannot talk over the telephone." Charles Taylor was the representative to the inves-tors. While Arych was busy in Guatemala, Taylor was dealing with one Texas art dealer who had breached the contract with Taylor and used the project to col-lect the investors' money for his own purpose.

This art dealer had stolen some of the inventory brought to the States by Taylor and privately sold them to some of his own contacts. Charles Taylor was aware of the jeopardy this dealer had put him into and as a result would move forward excluding this dealer from any future transactions. He hired an attorney who he trusted

To begin investigating this fraud and to study the extent of his fraudulent activities.

# CHAPTER XIV

# MORE DELAYS

Upon Taylor's arrival in Guatemala City, they immediately made plans to meet in Tegucigalpa, Capital of Honduras, with the former President of Honduras. The meeting was scheduled four weeks hence or late November 1976. Taylor returned to Texas and Arych to Guatemala City. This to protect the confidentiality of the excursion.

Charles Taylor was now contemplating how impressive this was to be. He thought of himself as the Lord Carnarvon, who financed Howard Carter in the seemingly endless discovery of the Tutankhamen's Tomb. Taylor paid entirely for Arych's expenses: travel, living and project expenses, the purchase of the artifacts which he purchased from Poco from the site in which they came or their origin years ago in Cerro El Bonete.

Taylor returned to Guatemala City late November and flew Sahsa-Tan Airlines ("stay at home, stay alive" airlines) to Tegucigalpa with Arych. They were met at the airport by the personal representatives of the President.

The meeting took place in the terminal headquarters of Sahsa-Tan Airlines with the past president of Honduras, his son-in-law, and his brother-in-law. Arych proceeded to make his presentation of over 100 pictures of the stone carvings. All this while he kept wondering why the past president and his family and why this meeting in the airport terminal. He then presented the former president with his presentation as a gift. The meeting lasted two hours entirely conducted in Spanish.

Arych was told he would have full military assistance in this endeavor. Taylor could not understand most of the conversation but enough to know that Arych had fully disclosed their findings and that his captured audience was completely aware of the potential of this discovery not only for themselves personally but also for their country. A future date was set for a second meeting on December 22, when a military expedition into Cerro El Bonete was to be scheduled.

Back at the hotel, Arych detailed the meeting contents to Taylor. Taylor asked, "Why did you disclose to them the locations and the findings in such detail?" Arych told him that all they wanted was to be recognized as the men who discovered this treasure. The artifacts would belong to each country. They discussed putting together a documentary and that the authorities from Honduras as well as Guatemala had ordered them to secrecy.

Taylor flew to San Pedro Sula where he got a flight into Miami and then back to Texas. Arych flew Sahsa-Tan Airlines to Guatemala City. While waiting Arych and Taylor spoke daily over the phone discussing the type of equipment required and how they would meet in Guatemala City in order to fly together back to Honduras.

Taylor, during one of the conversations, told Arych that since the project is taking so long, the investors he represented were becoming very dissatisfied. They cannot understand the delay. I explained the battles, the violence, the hostilities and the intrigue of Central America and the escalation of war since the project was undertaken. Since they do not read any of this in the papers or see it on the news, they find it hard to accept what I am telling them.

Also, I have been called to testify before the grand jury in Texas pertaining to the maverick art dealer who took so many investors' money. I've given voluntary statements, opened all our files to the authorities but they are convinced this operation is some sort of scam or fraud. We must publicize this quickly or we will fall into a political abyss in Texas. Arych listened attentively and then he spoke; "Charles, I am doing everything possible to move this along as quickly as I can. Once we have photographic proof of the existence of the cave system, this should solve the issue. Unfortunately, at this time the authorities will not permit publicity. They say for security reasons. But I will pursue this in a manner not to upset the authorities so that the doors will always remain open to us in particular to do the documentary we discussed."

# CHAPTER XV

# TEGUCIGALPA

Upon arrival in Tegucigalpa, Arych and Charles were met once again at the airport and quickly taken through customs to their hotel. The military were everywhere, including the U.S. Air Force troops. When asked what was going on, they were told that the military were on maneuvers. Repeatedly their scheduled meetings were postponed. We were advised to stay in their hotel for safety sake. They would be called when the meeting would be re-scheduled.

On the morning of December 24, a caller advised them that the President had flown to Guatemala to speak with Honduran President Laugerud regarding an emergency matter. The meeting would be rescheduled for the first two weeks of January 1977.

They were to wait for the time of this meeting. Arych and Charles witnessed a number of military vehicles and troops in the streets. No civilians were visible. All the businesses and houses were shuttered closed. They wondered if this was to be a coup d'etat by the communists.

# CHAPTER XVI

# 1977 ~ 1980

During the first week of January, they were collected by the former president's brother-in-law, Captain Figueroa, and taken to the Air Force Center at the International Airport in Tegucigalpa. They studied military maps of the area and made plans to land a DC 6 military transport on the tiny field runway at the ruins of Copan the next day.

The maps disclosed three Cerro El Benetes in the area of the ruins. One east, one west and the third 11 kilometers southwest of the ruins on the frontier with Guatemala.

Upon arrival at the air strip in Copan, an army unit met the plane, and they all began the search. By late afternoon, nothing was discovered in the first two centers investigated. The military had bombed shut the cave entrances 15 years earlier when they discovered guerrillas were using them to pass through the mountains from Honduras into Guatemala and vice versa. Everyone agreed to return to Teguci-galpa and arrange a second expedition the follow-ing day to the southwest site. Taylor, however, had to return to court in the USA and could not return with the expedition. This was to be a very difficult trial for Taylor.

The Hondurans military would not permit Arych to take his camera on the second flight. As the plane circled Cerro El Bonete, 11 kilometers southwest of the ruins of Copan, they were amazed at the modern looking roads which crisscrossed the Honduras fron-tier with Guatemala, all leading to the noted moun-tain. None of these roads were on the military maps. The military were equally amazed. It was apparent someone had dynamited several cave openings shut at El Bonete. BUT WHO?

As they circled a number of thatched roof struc-tures appeared on the side of the mountain at vari-ous heights and one on the top of the mountain as well. A closer examination revealed carved stones inside the structures. It was apparent that someone tried to get the ancient carvings out of there by air. Arych counted five streams coming out at the base of the mountain. There also was a limestone quarry at the base of the mountain. They checked their military maps once again. The clean cut and graded roads running from the west and the south toward the mountain were not on the maps.

The Honduran military took many photos of both the mountain as well as of the remote region surrounding it, Arych thought to himself this area is the site as described by Dr. Lopez and Grade. There were very few newly graded as well-maintained roads in Honduras or in Guatemala.

On their return route Captain Figueroa, the pilot and the former president's brother-in-law, instructed Arych to return to Guatemala City and wait for their call. At that time, he said, we will all go together to the cave and enter it once our military picture improves. He reminded Arych of the 200-mile common border with Nicaragua and the more than 100-mile border with El Salvador.

Both countries are at war. He told Arych that he could keep the pictures that they gave him. Arych was not permitted to publish the pictures or discuss the discovery with anyone. He instructed him also to not attempt to enter the site without military permission. The project is now considered top secret classification. Should the mountain contain the cultural treasures Arych described, and if it runs for 50 kilometers with many cave openings, it will take a full division of military to protect it.

He then asked Arych to call in a month to check on the status of the military situation with the Internal Security of Honduras. He assured Arych that his country was very grateful for his assistance in this discovery and that Arych and Taylor would get full recognition for the discovery as soon as it is safe and secure to do so.

Upon arrival in Guatemala City, Arych called Taylor and told him of his last inspection journey. He told of photographing the site and from the air was able to determine this was Dr. Lopez/Grade's site. Taylor agreed to meet him in Guatemala City in the following week to determine the next step.

It was early February when Charles returned. They carefully examined the photographs taken from the DC 6. They made additional plans on how they were to photograph the inside of the caves and their discovery.

They met in Guatemala City with Colonel Smyth and Lemos. Colonel Lemos asked to borrow the photographs for several days for their military people to review. The pictures were never returned. Arych was refused by the Honduras military when he requested a second set. Arych called once each month, as asked to do so by Captain Figueroa. The answer was always the same. Not yet, our battles are worse than when you were here, but be patient, we will enter the site together with plenty of time for exploration and the documentary of the discovery.

This process went on and on throughout 1977 and 1978. In June of 1977, the Mayor of Jocotan's secretary, Feliz, who was in charge of the money from the sale of the stones was found murdered.

Poco disappeared at this time. He was placed on the CIA's Most Wanted List by Colonel Lemos. When Poco was found, he was arrested and charged with crimes against archeology.

Newspaper headlines at this time: Massacre in Jocotan. The police were looking for two men for murdering ten Indians. These men may have escaped across the frontier into Honduras. These two men were Poco's brothers.

Arych continued to receive expenses from Taylor, purchasing artifacts from various people associated with the village of Jocotan. He was shipping them to Brussels, Israel, and England, The Cayman Islands, Texas, and California.

During this time Taylor was in Europe meeting with Dr. Michael Ripinsky, considered an expert art historian, archeologist, and appraiser. He met with major art dealers, collectors, Auction houses and museums in an effort to determine the market for the treasures. Suddenly, one day, the final 200 sculptures which Arych and Taylor had purchased were confiscated by the Department of Archeology in Guatemala City.

Arych continued his research to understand what was suddenly going on with the discovery. He discovered one official document from the Municipality of Chiquimula (Jocotan's state) which provided Grade (now wanted for many years for looting) the right to explore and research poisonous plants. A second document gave approval to Grade to use Poco of Jocotan as his guide.

Arych kept on thinking and researching. He could not understand why a notable guide such as Grade was traveling to Jocotan in Central America to hunt poisonous plants? Why would such a notable require Poco to guide him? What was their relationship? What were they really doing together?

It started to make some sense that Poco was arrested and then let go only to be approved to be a guide for a wanted looter. Dr. Lopez was mentioned in several of the documents, but they were blacked out in all of the U.S. government files. Why? Arych wondered if he was in the middle of a once in a lifetime discovery or a major fraud or both.

Arych started to think and believe that he must be quiet and careful with whom he talks, since it is now evident that something sinister is going on.

# 1978

The first part of 1978, Taylor returned to Guatemala City and purchased thousands of dollars in expeditionary equipment. Dr. Lopez and Grade had now agreed to take Arych and Taylor to an ancient ceremonial center near the border of Copan.

During the journey, their truck broke down, once with engine trouble and then flat tires. With no spare tires available they were forced to walk and climb the mountain in the heat and were near exhaustion. It now appeared to Arych that Grade was a master of deceit and intrigue. They never saw one cave. They saw anything!

Taylor, however, decided to purchase more of the artifacts prior to March when he was called by a Grand Jury subpoena in New York. Scotland Yard required a statement from him in April of this same year. As a result, Taylor sent his son James to Guatemala City to keep watch on this business and on everything.

James took an apartment next door to Arych. One night, James heard Arych and Dr. Lopez shouting at each other. Arych threatened Dr. Lopez that if he did not take him to the site where he was looting that he would expose him to the authorities. Dr. Lopez attempted to strangle Arych, but in the process, the doors to their rooms were slammed shut.

On June 3rd, James flew to Los Angeles to wait for the results of the testing being performed on some of the artifacts. The next day, June 4, Arych's apartment was raided by the police and Arych was arrested. He was allowed a court appointed attorney, Fernando Hurtado. Finally, after two months in jail, Arych was released.

While he was in prison, at Arych's request, Atty. Hurtado wrote a letter to Taylor stating: "This letter is to inform you of the details Arych Ben-Ami. He has been taken by the police at his apartment because they were notified that Arych had various pre-Columbian artifacts. These artifacts were carefully examined by an archeological expert and declared them to be authentic. In this country, the charges of possessing archeological pieces without proper documents are considered criminal. This is why Mr. Ben-Ami was required to spend two months in jail. As his attorney I was able to get him free after two months and he is allowed to stay in Guatemala and can do what he wishes in this country."

Sincerely yours,

**Fernando Hurtado**

# 1979

Determined more now, than ever, Arych returned to the village of Copan, hired two guides, and started his trek to Cerro El Bonete. After three days of searching in the area, he finally found a main entrance into a cave. Just as he was about to enter the cave, one of the guides advised him he was a national police agent with the FBI and his orders were to return Arych to Tegucigalpa, to the Interpol Headquarters. The guides instructions were to stay with Arych until he found the entrance and then return him to Interpol.

Once again Arych wanted photographs to prove his discovery. He was not permitted to take even one photograph of the hieroglyphic walls on either side of the entrance. He was under arrest.

At Interpol Headquarters in Tegucigalpa, Arych's passport, equipment including his camera were confiscated. The next morning Colonel Figueroa visited Arych and told him he was sorry for the inconvenience however he had to insist on no publicity of the discovery. He repeated that the government in Honduras had more than it could handle at the time. When the government felt it was time, they would indeed all enter the caves together. He then told Arych he would be released to be returned to the US.

He said once more to be patient because it would not be much longer, and they will all enter the subterranean together. Your passport and personal property will be returned to you at the airport upon landing in the States.

Once more, Arych pressed for photographs explaining to him that he needed evidence for the investors and for all of the people who believed in him in this venture. Again, the answer was, "no, we cannot do that. We do not want the place known."

Arych reminded him that after Dr. Lopez showed it to Arych, Arych showed it to the Honduran's. "No." replied the Colonel. Once again critical events were occurring in Honduras, and it was too risky to permit any documentary at this time. If Arych wanted to ever evidence the discovery, he had to obey the Colonel.

The Colonel went on to tell Arych that this is his country and if Arych behaved he would continue to be welcomed. "If not, well – you can imagine what trouble you would be in. We do not want or need any publicity. This is a "top secret" matter. When you return to the States you will call us once a month, and we will advise you of our progress in resolving our Internal Security matters. When we are ready, we will all enter the caves together, for many weeks, and you can then arrange the filming of your documentary."

For the first half of 1979, Arych continued to call Honduras. During this time Charles Taylor continued his quest of seeking authentication and appraisals on the artifacts they had recovered.

In April of 1979, Taylor testified before the Grand Jury in Texas. During this time Dr. Ripinsky authenticated 25 sculptures. His report concluded that there was no question that these artifacts were authentic.

In May of 1979 a full-scale war erupted in Nicaragua. In July, Nicaragua President Somosa resigned.

During the summer of 1979, over 200 tablets were lost or damaged in shipping. Some were destroyed in a warehouse in London.

In August, Arych testified before the Grand Jury in Texas. He and Taylor plotted Arych's return to Honduras to get evidence. Taylor gave Arych money to stay for two weeks. He had to bring back evidence. This seemed the only way to prove their case.

Meanwhile, Dr. Carmichael of the London museum, examined the collection of stone carvings. During this time, Taylor pays $35,000 for the art appraisals and authentications.

For tax purposes, Taylor donates $225,000 worth of artifacts to one of the museums based upon the appraisals and authentications of value by Dr. Ripinsky.

# 1980

In February 1980, Charles Taylor, Arych Ben-Ami, and the Texas art dealers were indicted by a Federal Grand Jury for conspiracy to defraud. The Texas art dealers agreed to testify against Taylor and Arych in exchange for two-and one-half years of suspended sentences.

Their testimony stated that Taylor represented to them in 1975, and, in turn, to their investors that the stone carvings were not only in their opinion authentic but that they had been authenticated. They were indicted on 2 to 6 counts of conspiracy to defraud.

In June of this year, Arych, now penniless, and held in a Federal prison since February, was unable to post bail is now represented by a court appointed attorney. He refused to tell anyone where he was. Prior to Taylor's trial, Arych was told to plea bargain guilty to 2 of the 6 counts pending against him for conspiracy to defraud. He was threatened with 5 years on each count or a total of 30 years. If he did this, he would receive a total of two-and-one-half years and be eligible for parole in eight months. He would not be required to testify against Taylor, but he was not allowed to tell Taylor of his plea agreement.

During this same time period, Taylor was released on his own recognizance. Prior to Taylor's trial, Dr. Ripinsky was brought in for extended conferences with Taylor's counsel. In pre-trial discussions, the Defense Counsel outlined to the Government prosecutors his testimony. Dr. Ripinsky was told that if he was used in this trial, they would find a way to destroy his testimony.

Soon after the last meeting with the prosecutors, Dr. Ripinsky was approached by the IRS posing as art dealers, asking him to obtain a pre-date on a donation of artwork to both the Los Angeles Museum of Art, and the University of California.

The museums supplied Dr. Ripinsky with back dated receipts in return for their art donations (This was a common practice at the time). As a result of this transaction, Dr. Ripinsky was charged, convicted, and sent to prison. A brilliant career destroyed. Also, destroyed were all of Taylor's appraisals and authentications.

Throughout Taylor's trial, not one of Taylor's expert witnesses were used. The only defense his counsel presented was Taylor's good reputation, based on the words of ten lawyers and a judge as well as Taylor's own testimony.

The US Attorney used the Texas art dealers (guilty of fraud), the disgruntled Texas investors, 3 expert witnesses who testified they did not believe the tablets on exhibit were real historical artifacts, and most damaging of all, the government of Guatemala provided in person Poco Sanchez and Dr. Julio Lopez, who stated that he and his associates had carved the tablets.

Also, Dr. Munoz testified that Poco Sanchez had carved them from his imagination and the Director of Guatemala approved the exportation of the carved tablets as decorative works of art and reproduction.

Throughout the trial, the prosecutor indicated to the jury that Arych would testify, knowing full well they made a deal with Arych and that Arych would not testify unless called to do so by the defense.

The jury returned a verdict of guilty on four of the six counts. Taylor was sentenced to six concurrent terms of two-and one-half years each.

After paying most of the investors back out of his own pocket and exhausting his pro se appeals, Taylor served fourteen months in prison and was released on parole in 1984. He did not pay back the Texas art dealer's investors. When released he was destitute and diagnosed with lung cancer.

Arych set forth to understand what went wrong. He was so wrapped up in proving his discovery, he did not see the forest for the trees.

When Taylor donated the first pieces to museums and took a tax deduction, the IRS asked the US Attorney to investigate a way to shut down Arych and

Taylor. The FBI spent four years investigating and the result was that they could not certify that the artifacts were real or not. Even with a good case, the trial itself shut down the operation, since no one would continue their interest in the artifacts.

The IRS was not going to allow the wealthy US art collectors, who purchased the artifacts at low costs, to export them from Guatemala as decorative art only to later be authenticated by distinguished appraisers such as Dr. Ripinsky for three times more, in order for them to donate the artifacts to major museums and take a healthy tax deduction on each piece.

The reality was that Dr. Lopez who used Arych and Taylor to initiate the art scam and followed the delivery of the carvings into the United States and Europe began thinking that Arych and Taylor were becoming too high profile and wanted them shut down before they destroyed a good thing.

Arych thought of Dr. Lopez. He wondered just how much a part did he play in the overall scheme of things. Meanwhile, further investigations revealed Dr. Lopez was not only a looter, but it was revealed that he was a CIA agent and DEA informant.

Dr. Lopez employed Grade in the early sixties when he owned a ranch in Belize and hired him to end a problem on the ranch when jaguars were killing his cattle. They became close friends during this period.

Grade was of Italian and Indian descent and spoke all the Mayan dialects. Grade was running liquor in Costa Rica when the police caught him. He called Dr. Lopez who, with another CIA agent, paid $5,000 to arrange for Grade to escape from the Costa Rican jail.

Grade was notably Central America's foremost hunting guide. He had been written up in many books and magazines. He acknowledged having 71 children with as many women. When he walked throughout Belize many a child called him papa. Sports Illustrated was banned for six months in Belize for printing the article. Grade died in 1990 at the age of 72.

It was now apparent that Dr. Lopez, Grade and Poco were fronting for the sale of the artifacts before the earthquake and discovery made through the infra-red cameras.

It was when Arych went to the government with his story and both Col. Smythe and Col. Lemos became involved that the guerrilla warfare engulfed the caves and became even more dangerous. Everyone wanted a piece of the pie.

Everyone involved with the sale of tablets and other artifacts to Arych, and Taylor were from Jocotan; all were murdered. It is said that one Indian remains, and he is in hiding, but continues to work for Col. Lemos. Poco Sanchez was shot and killed in 1989. No one knows who killed him, but it is rumored that the greed among the guerillas from the surrounding villages of Jocotan were responsible.

As of the date of our last investigation Col. Smythe and Dr. Lopez are drinking buddies and meet regularly. The Colonel controls the Air Force and also has been head of the International Airport from 1975.

Col. Lemos, Minister of the Interior and Internal Security from 1975 through 1980, did not want the centers publicized until he became President. His attempted coup in 1989 failed. For this he was sentenced to ten years in prison. He served ten months. Today he is manager of a fertilization plant owned by one of the ruling families of Guatemala, Rodrigo Guerra.

Guerra, who is also CIA trained and educated in France and the USA continues to control all the major trucking and road building equipment companies including all military trucks and equipment. Guerra is a longtime friend of Dr. Lopez, Col. Smythe, and Col. Lemos.

Attorney Fernando Hurtado's father was head of the Supreme Court of Guatemala and drew up the contracts for Arych and Taylor. In 1991 he was appointed to the powerful position of Minister of the Interior, replacing Col Lemos.

The man who was responsible for shipping the artifacts for Arych was known as Santa Marina. He is now an important businessman who also owns the Popol Vuh museum where many a wealthy art collector has visited and discreetly would inquire about a particular artifact – only to have that particular artifact disappear and later reappear as part of his collection. The artifact would then be replaced by another, and Hurtado would take care of the paperwork.

To be the looter, was to be making money. The looters had CIA contacts, control of the airport, trucking, and Internal Security and of course the pre-Columbian museum.

The Honduran Arrellano family owned the airlines, major hotels, and travel agencies. Since 1978 they purchased up the land near and around the caves, driving off the Indians. They dynamited many cave openings only to seal them from discovery and further looting.

The Indians in this story have told Arych of their living in fear of the day the government will arrest them and take their land and their ancestral caves.

Arych has been in the caves, witnessed the high, dry limestone alters and carvings on the walls. His belief is that perhaps in 1992, the 500th anniversary of the discovery of the Americas, they would publicly announce the discovery of the caves. This did not happen.

However, Arych wonders: How can they discover something that was discovered years ago. Why didn't the Department of Archeology and the world learn about it then?

Arych knows that all of the men in this story possess codices. However, only Arych, and one other friend have a codex which has passed the Carbon 14 test (the age of the bark/paper) and the migration test (the date the ink was placed on the bark/paper).

These tests were completed by two United States University laboratories. None of the others know about these tests.

Dr. Lopez was once asked about his codex and what he was told when he presented it to the Smithsonian for evaluation.

What would it be worth, if authenticated? He said it would be priceless. His current offer was already at seven million dollars.

It is rumored that there is a codex at the Vatican. In 1990 the European Community pledged nine hundred million dollars to develop a tourism program which they called "The Mayan World". It didn't happen.

Charles Taylor's last words were that the verdict is in, but the evidence is still out. This story may be Charles Taylor and Arych Ben-Ami last appeal for the truth.

The exploration, inventory and publication of the centers may one day right a grievous wrong. This day may never come in time for Arych to realize the success of his discovery.

He returned to Israel with his codex. Arych would never be able to publicize his ownership or share them with the outside world.

He returned to the home of his deceased parents. Last heard he was living alone with the memories of such an unbelievable tale. No one knows where he is in Israel, or if he is even alive.

# ABOUT THE AUTHOR

Loving and inspiring wife, mother, grandmother, and great grandmother.

Barbara Shaw Miller moved to Arizona in 1971. She became a licensed Real Estate agent in New Jersey in1970 prior to moving to Arizona in 1971. While a resident of Metuchen, New Jersey, she was employed in New York city for Associated Merchandise Corp. as Exec. Assistant to the President of the company.

Graduated from Katherine Gibbs Business School, Park Avenue, New York City, as well as Completing several courses at New York University School of Retailing.

She obtained a real estate license in AZ immediately wherein it was decided Real Estate Appraising was preferable to sales. As a member of the Society of Real Estate Appraisers' she earned the SRA and SRPA designations. Barbara served as President of the Phoenix chapter.

She was asked by Prentice Hall, Institute of Business Planning to write a book on the workings of the Appraisal process, *"Real Estate Appraisers Kit"* was published in1983.

When Western Saving sold to D. K. Ludwig, in addition to her appraisal department responsibilities, was assigned to be the Project manager for a development project at Westlake Village. Ca. The project consisted of a hotel, restaurant, and office building.

At her retirement she was asked by the former Oil Minister of Vietnam to travel to China and Vietnam to demonstrate the requirement for a welcomed project submitted for financing a loan by the American banks. In Beijing she attended a class conducted by the head of the College, Professor Han. He asked her to be an Honorary Professor of the Beijing Business and Arts College in 1998.

Later, on this same trip, she visited Dalian China, where she was presented a Letter of Appointment by the Dalian Xinghai Bay Development and Construction Administration Centre as a consultant for overseas investments.

She was a member of the World League for Freedom and Democracy, headquartered in Taipei. Taiwan. Since her travels were extended, she visited Japan and South Korea.

In Japan, she was invited to become a member of the Japan Korean Buddhist Welfare Association headed by Noboru Kakinuma, who also invited Tom Miller to be a member of the Association which continues under the leadership of Masakasu Nikajima. The Millers are still appointed members of this Association.

Barbara enjoyed golf and as a member of the Az Biltmore Club she also played tennis.

She loves to laugh, and for entertainment, she enjoys plays and movies.

Most of all she loves her family. Her husband, Tom, and daughter Katie are in her heart forever.